Hi Diddle Diddle

A Book of Mother Goose Rhymes

Pictures by NOLA LANGNER

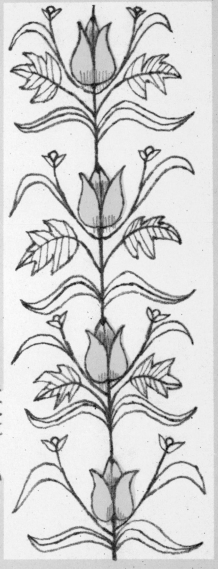

NEW YORK • TORONTO • LONDON • AUCKLAND • SYDNEY • TOKYO

Mother Goose rhymes in this book

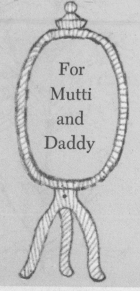

For
Mutti
and
Daddy

Big A, Little a	Georgie Porgie
Simple Simon	There Was a Little Girl
Little Miss Muffet	When Jack's a Very Good Boy
Little Jack Horner	Jack and Jill
Old Mother Hubbard	Little Bo-peep
Hi Diddle Diddle	Little Boy Blue
Pussy Cat, Pussy Cat	A Diller, a Dollar
Six Little Mice	Early to Bed
I Love Little Pussy	Sing a Song of Sixpence
What Are Little Girls Made Of?	As I Went over the Water
What Are Little Boys Made Of?	Humpty Dumpty
Mary, Mary Quite Contrary	My Black Hen
Peter, Peter Pumpkin Eater	Higglety, Pigglety, Pop!
Lucy Locket	Twinkle, Twinkle, Little Star

5th printing .... October 1971

Printed in the U.S.A.

Star Light, Star Bright

Rock-a-bye Baby

There Was an Old Woman
Who Lived in a Shoe

The King of France

Little Jumping Joan

Jack Be Nimble

Jerry Hall

Jack Sprat

Rain on the Green Grass

Rain, Rain, Go Away

Pease Porridge Hot

Here We Go Round
the Mulberry Bush

Mary Had a Little Lamb

I'll Tell You a Story

Big A, little a
　　Bouncing B!
The cat's in the cupboard,
　　And can't see me.

Can you say your ABC?
A B C D E F G H I J K L M N O P Q R S T U V W X Y Z

Simple Simon met a pieman,
  Going to the fair.
Said Simple Simon to the pieman,
  "Let me taste your ware."

Said the pieman to Simple Simon,
  "Show me first your penny."
Said Simple Simon to the pieman,
  "Indeed, I have not any."

Simple Simon went a-fishing,
 For to catch a whale.
All the water he could find
 Was in his mother's pail.

He went to ride a spotted cow,
 That had a spotted calf.
She threw him down upon the ground,
 Which made the people laugh.

Little Miss Muffet
Sat on a tuffet,
    Eating her curds and whey.
Along came a spider,
Who sat down beside her,
    And frightened Miss Muffet away.

Little Jack Horner
Sat in a corner
    Eating a Christmas pie.
He put in his thumb,
And pulled out a plum,
    And said, "What a good boy am I."

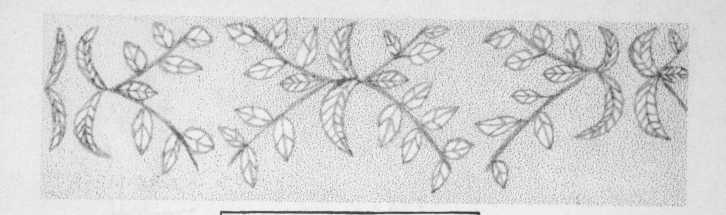

Old Mother Hubbard
Went to the cupboard,
To get her poor dog a bone.
But when she got there
The cupboard was bare.
And so the poor dog had none.

She went to the tailor's
To buy him a coat.
But when she came back
He was riding a goat.

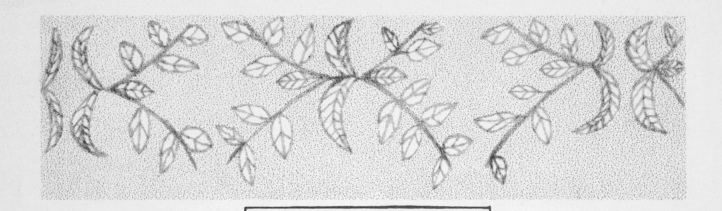

She went to the hatter's
    To buy him a hat.
But when she came back
    He was feeding the cat.

She went to the barber's
    To buy him a wig.
But when she came back
    He was dancing a jig.

Hi diddle diddle,

The cat and the fiddle,

　　The cow jumped over the moon.

The little dog laughed

To see such fun,

　　And the dish ran away with the spoon.

Pussy cat, pussy cat, where have you been?
I've been to London to visit the queen.
Pussy cat, pussy cat, what did you there?
I frightened a little mouse under her chair.

Six little mice sat down to spin.
Pussy passed by and she peeped in.

"What are you doing, my little men?"
"Weaving coats for gentlemen."

"Shall I come in and cut off your threads?"
"No, no, Mistress Pussy, you'd bite off our heads."

I love little pussy,
    Her coat is so warm.
And if I don't hurt her,
    She'll do me no harm.

So I'll not pull her tail,
    Nor drive her away.
But pussy and I
    Very gently will play.

She shall sit by my side,
    And I'll give her some food.
And pussy will love me
    Because I am good.

What are little girls made of?
What are little girls made of?
   Sugar and spice
   And everything nice,
That's what little girls are made of.

What are little boys made of?
What are little boys made of?
   Snips and snails
   And puppy-dogs' tails,
That's what little boys are made of.

Mary, Mary,
Quite contrary,
   How does your garden grow?
With silver bells
And cockle shells
   And pretty maids all in a row.

Peter, Peter, pumpkin eater,
Had a wife and couldn't keep her.
He put her in a pumpkin shell,
And there he kept her very well.

Lucy Locket lost her pocket.
Kitty Fisher found it.
Nothing in it, nothing in it,
But the ribbon round it.

Georgie, Porgie, pudding and pie,
Kissed the girls and made them cry.
When the boys came out to play,
Georgie Porgie ran away.

There was a little girl,
And she had a little curl
    Right in the middle of her forehead.
When she was good,
She was very very good.
    But when she was bad she was horrid.

When Jack's a very good boy,
    He shall have cake and custard.
But when he does nothing but cry,
    He shall have nothing but mustard.

Jack and Jill
Went up the hill
   To fetch a pail of water.
Jack fell down
And broke his crown,
   And Jill came tumbling after.

Little Bo-peep
Has lost her sheep
    And can't tell where to find them.
Let them alone
And they'll come home,
    Wagging their tails behind them.

Little Boy Blue, come blow your horn,
The sheep's in the meadow, the cow's in the corn.
But where is the little boy tending the sheep?
He's under the haystack fast asleep.

A diller, a dollar, a ten o'clock scholar!
What makes you come so soon?
You used to come at ten o'clock,
But now you come at noon.

Early to bed,
Early to rise,
Makes a man healthy,
Wealthy, and wise.

Sing a song of sixpence,
    A pocket full of rye.
Four and twenty blackbirds
    Baked in a pie.

When the pie was opened,
    The birds began to sing.
Now wasn't that a dainty dish,
    To set before the king?

The king was in the counting-house,
  Counting out his money.
The queen was in the parlor,
  Eating bread and honey.

The maid was in the garden,
  Hanging out the clothes.
Along came a blackbird
  And snipped off her nose.

As I went over the water,
    The water went over me.
I saw two little blackbirds
    Sitting in a tree.

One called me rascal,
    And one called me thief,
I took up my little black stick
    And knocked out all their teeth.

Humpty Dumpty sat on a wall.

Humpty Dumpty had a great fall.

All the king's horses

And all the king's men

Couldn't put Humpty Dumpty together again.

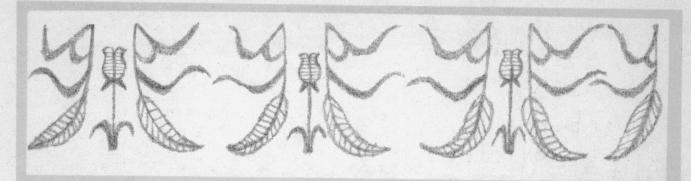

Higglety, pigglety, my black hen,
She lays eggs for gentlemen.
Sometimes nine and sometimes ten,
Higglety, pigglety, my black hen.

Higglety, pigglety, pop!
The dog has eaten the mop.
The pig's in a hurry,
The cat's in a flurry,
Higglety, pigglety, pop!

Twinkle, twinkle, little star,
How I wonder what you are!
Up above the world so high
Like a diamond in the sky.

Star light, star bright,
First star I see tonight,
I wish I may, I wish I might,
Have the wish I wish tonight.

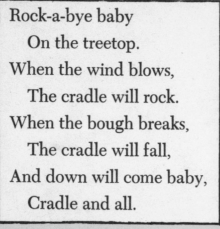

Rock-a-bye baby
     On the treetop.
When the wind blows,
     The cradle will rock.
When the bough breaks,
     The cradle will fall,
And down will come baby,
     Cradle and all.

There was an old woman who lived in a shoe.
She had so many children she didn't know what to do.
She gave them some soup without any bread.
She spanked them all soundly and put them to bed.

The king of France went up the hill,
  With forty thousand men.
The king of France came down the hill,
  And never went up again.

Here am I,
Little jumping Joan.
When nobody's with me,
I'm all alone.

Jack be nimble,
Jack be quick,
Jack jump over
The candle stick.

Jerry Hall
He is so small,
A rat could eat him,
Hat and all.

Jack Sprat
Could eat no fat.
His wife could eat no lean.
And so between the two of them
They licked the platter clean.

Rain on the green grass,
And rain on the tree,
Rain on the house-top,
But not on me.

Rain, rain, go away,
Come again another day.
Little Johnny wants to play.

Pease porridge hot,
     Pease porridge cold,
Pease porridge in the pot,
     Nine days old.

Some like it hot,
     Some like it cold,
Some like it in the pot,
     Nine days old.

Here we go round the mulberry bush,
  The mulberry bush, the mulberry bush.
Here we go round the mulberry bush,
  On a cold and frosty morning.

This is the way we brush our hair,
  Brush our hair, brush our hair,
This is the way we brush our hair,
  On a cold and frosty morning.

This is the way we clap our hands,
Clap our hands, clap our hands.
This is the way we clap our hands,
On a cold and frosty morning.

This is the way we stamp our feet,
Stamp our feet, stamp our feet.
This is the way we stamp our feet,
On a cold and frosty morning.

Mary had a little lamb,
Its fleece was white as snow.
And everywhere that Mary went
The lamb was sure to go.

It followed her to school one day,
 That was against the rule.
It made the children laugh and play
 To see a lamb in school.

I'll tell you a story
About Jack-a-Nory.
And now my story's begun.

I'll tell you another
About his brother.
And now my story is done.